S0-CMS-595

Mary
Hollingsworth

Rainbows

illustrated by
Leah Palmer Preiss

The C.R. Gibson Company • Norwalk, Connecticut

Every effort has been made to trace the ownership of all copyrighted material.
Unless otherwise attributed, Bible quotations are from *The Everyday Bible, New
Century Version,* copyrighted © 1987 by Worthy Publishing, Irving, Texas 75039.
Page 11 "Trust" by Betsey Kline from *Sourcebook of Poetry* by Al Bryant, published
by Zondervan Publishing House, Grand Rapids, MI copyright © 1967.
Published by The C.R. Gibson Company, Norwalk, CT 06856
ISBN 0-8378-1877-X
GB507
Printed in the U.S.A.

My Heart Leaps Up

My Heart leaps up when I behold
A rainbow in the sky:
So was it when my life began;
So is it now I am a man;
So be it when I shall grow old,
Or let me die!
The Child is the father of the Man;
And I could wish my days to be
Bound each to each by natural piety.

William Wordsworth

Stepping Out

Okay, Lord, I'm stepping out here now. Are You there? Will You catch me if I fall? You know I've never tried anything like this before, and I'm scared. I'm plumb white-knuckled, silly scared.

I'm testing You, Lord. I know we're not supposed to test You, but if we don't test what You've said, how will we ever have faith? I admit it. I'm stepping out here on faith, and I'm not sure what I'll do if my faith doesn't hold me up. What will I do if I fall flat on my face? Will I be able to get up again? I don't know...I just don't know.

My friends encourage me to try new things, to use the talents You've given me. That's easy for them to say. They don't have to stand up here in front of all those staring faces. They don't have to sing that high note at the end of the song with a mouth that feels as if it's full of cotton and a throat totally closed with nervous tension. Their palms aren't sweaty.

There's my friend on the front row. She doesn't look nervous, and she's done this lots of times. She's the one who got me into this mess anyway. Well, she knows me better than anyone else, and she's confident I can do it. Maybe she's right.

I'll try, Lord. I'm going to walk out on that stage, announce my song and give it my best shot. I'm stepping out here now. And I'm sure You're there. I can see You smiling at me through my friend. Maybe this won't be so bad after all. They're applauding. I trust You, Lord, but don't let her stop smiling, okay?

*T*rust

*S*ure, it takes a lot of courage
To put things in God's hands,
To give ourselves completely,
Our lives, our hopes, our plans;
To follow where He leads us
And make His will our own,
But all it takes is foolishness
To go the way alone.

 Betsey Kline

*I*n God I have put my trust.
Psalm 56:4 KJV

Her Right To Joy

There she was again, standing at the altar, smiling at a man that she loved and to whom she was giving the rest of her life. And she meant it. This was no sham. This was Frances.

I sang my song and waited for my next cue as the minister talked of commitment and lifelong promises. My mind questioned, "But how long will life be this time for Frances?" Three other times Frances had pledged her love "until death do us part" and three times death had, indeed, parted them.

Most women would have just given up in despair and sunk into a mire of self-pity. But this was Frances. And there she was again, standing at the altar, not willing to give up on life. She was not willing to declare defeat in the search for happiness and love. She had taken up her faith, gathered up her hope and found love once more.

She claimed her right to joy.

A Birthday

My heart is like a singing bird
Whose nest is in a watered shoot;
My heart is like an apple tree
Whose boughs are bent with thickset fruit;
My heart is like a rainbow shell
That paddles in a halcyon sea;
My heart is gladder than all these
Because my love is come to me.

Raise me a dais of silk and down;
Hang it with vair and purple dyes;
Carve it in doves, and pomegranates,
And peacocks with a hundred eyes;
Work it in gold and silver grapes,
In leaves and silver fleurs-de-lys;
Because the birthday of my life
Is come, my love is come to me.

Christina Rossetti

My Choices

I'd rather be me than anyone else I know.
I'd rather laugh than cry.
I'd rather trust than be suspicious.
I'd rather hope than despair.
I'd rather believe in God than try to believe in nothing.
I'd rather love than hate.
I'd rather have faith than be afraid.
I'd rather be learning on the outside than dying on the inside.
I'd rather sing than mourn.
I'd rather be optimistic than worried.
I'd rather live with myself than someone I don't like.
I'd rather have good friends than be a hermit.
I'd rather look for good in people than look for evil.
I'd rather ride than walk.
I'd rather pray than feel helpless.
I'd rather read a good book than watch a good movie.
I'd rather eat popcorn than read a good book.
And I'd rather write than eat.

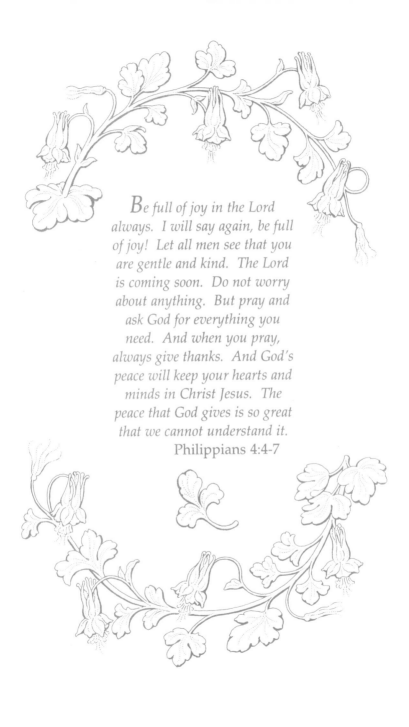

Be full of joy in the Lord
always. I will say again, be full
of joy! Let all men see that you
are gentle and kind. The Lord
is coming soon. Do not worry
about anything. But pray and
ask God for everything you
need. And when you pray,
always give thanks. And God's
peace will keep your hearts and
minds in Christ Jesus. The
peace that God gives is so great
that we cannot understand it.

Philippians 4:4-7

I Wandered Lonely as a Cloud

I wandered lonely as a cloud
That floats on high o'er vales and hills,
When all at once I saw a crowd,
A host, of golden daffodils;
Beside the lake, beneath the trees,
Fluttering and dancing in the breeze.

Continuous as the stars that shine
And twinkle on the milky way,
They stretched in never-ending line
Along the margin of a bay:
Ten thousand saw I at a glance,
Tossing their heads in sprightly dance.

The waves beside them danced; but they
Outdid the sparkling waves in glee;
A poet could not but be gay,
In such a jocund company;
I gazed—and gazed—but little thought
What wealth the show to me had brought:

For oft, when on my couch I lie
In vacant or in pensive mood,
They flash upon that inward eye
Which is the bliss of solitude;
And then my heart with pleasure fills,
And dances with the daffodils.

 William Wordsworth

The Happiest Heart

The happiest heart that ever beat
Was in some quiet breast
That found the common daylight sweet,
And left to Heaven the rest.

 John Vance Cheney

Emma

Emma was 89 years old, and when you asked her what she did for a living, she answered cheerily, "I take care of old people."

I was invited to Emma's for dinner one Friday evening. When I arrived, I found a dilapidated old two-story frame house in a poorer section of Pittsburgh. I knocked on the door, and one of Emma's "old people" let me into the dark living room. Emma came from the kitchen to give me a smile and a hug.

Soon Emma pulled the twine that rang the little bell at the top of the stairs, and her tenants began to descend for dinner. They came with canes. They came slowly, holding hands or helping each other. But they all came smiling. They took turns hugging Emma and introducing themselves to me. Then Emma guided me to the seat of honor at the end of the shaky, old table, and we enjoyed a pleasant dinner, laughing and telling stories.

During the course of the evening, I learned that Emma's friends were castaways of society. They were homeless, street people Emma had adopted so they wouldn't starve on her doorstep. They were lonely, helpless and hopeless. Emma cared for them with her own money and never asked help from anyone else. The fact is, most of Emma's old people were younger than she was. And most of them were in better health than Emma, too.

Emma could have decided she had earned a rest and sat easily rocking away the rest of her life. She could have chosen to be an old person, too, rather than taking care of old people. She could have been the victim rather than the victorious. Emma was no ordinary lady though. She was the hope of the hopeless, help of the helpless and a friend of the lonely.

Shared joy is double joy and shared sorrow is half-sorrow.

Swedish proverb

Opportunity

I am the blind man you pass on the street
Selling my papers for something to eat;
I am the beggar who knocks on your door
Pleading a morsel or crumb—nothing more.

I am the hitchhiker shivering, cold,
Thumbing a ride with cumbersome load;
I am the widow whose loneliness cries
For quiet compassion in warm, friendly eyes.

I am the cripple whose arthritic hand
Reaches to touch you...can you understand?
I am the infant whose parents have fled,
Caring not whether I'm living or dead.

I am the homeless, rejected and poor;
Hear with your heart my lonely adjure:
"Lend me your comfort, share your kind smile,
Just linger a moment or chat for a while."

Love one another as I have loved you.
John 15:12 KJV

How green under the boughs it is!
How thick the tremulous sheep-cries come!

Sometimes a child will cross the glade
To take his nurse his broken toy;
Sometimes a thrush flit overhead
Deep in her unknown day's employ.

Here at my feet what wonders pass,
What endless, active life is here!
What blowing daisies, fragrant grass!
An air stirr'd forest, fresh and clear...

 Matthew Arnold

Nurse's Song

When the voices of children are heard on the green
And laughing is heard on the hill,
My heart is at rest within my breast
And everything else is still.

 William Blake

A Thing of Beauty

A thing of beauty is a joy for ever:
Its loveliness increases; it will never
Pass into nothingness; but still will keep
A bower quiet for us, and a sleep
Full of sweet dreams, and health, and quiet
breathing.

 John Keats

*B*lind Man's Bluff

Leonard and Jack Burford and their sister Mable were all three blind from birth through heredity. A tragedy, you say? Not to them.

Dr. Leonard Burford was an extraordinary professor of choral music at Abilene Christian College for many years where he directed the a cappela chorus of 70 or more voices. He could call the offending singer by name and identify which note was wrong and what the note should have been. He was a living, breathing phenomenon. And he was loved by all who knew him. Today, the Leonard Burford Music Center is a tribute to his influence.

Jack and Mable lived with Leonard in their tri-level home in south Abilene. They had converted part of their home into a professional sound studio, complete with microphones, sound-proofing, piano and all the trimmings. The middle level of the house was transformed into the sound control booth where Jack worked as the engineer to produce high-quality recordings. It was fascinating to stand in that room full of little knobs, switches and dials and watch that blind gentleman fiddle with them masterfully to produce such pure and refined sounds.

Mable was involved in many phases of the recorded productions, from handling the business dealings to making their home / studio a welcome place for friends or clients.

The Burfords' neighbors, I am told, were often a bit disconcerted by their blind friends. One of the brothers' hobbies was woodworking in the other half of their basement, using powerful electrical machinery to produce fine furniture. What disturbed his neighbors was that he worked such late hours in a dark basement.

The neighbors also found it strange to hear the Burfords out mowing their lawn at night, preferring the cool of the evening to the heat of the midday sun.

These wonderful people had not only learned to cope with their blindness, but they had learned to capitalize on it. Lacking sight, they fine-tuned their audio abilities and physical dexterities. They developed outstanding people skills and leadership abilities.

I've thought of the Burfords often through the years—the visits I made to their home, the work I did with them in their studio, their presence on the college campus, their influence on me and other students and their incredibly positive approach to life. In many ways, their blindness opened my eyes but through the heart and mind. I learned that trust in God is not based on what we see around us but what we know of Him and His promises.

I can do all things through Christ because He gives me strength.
Philippians 4:13

Love Is Stronger Than Death

Love is stronger than death. I know it's true because my grandmother has been gone for thirty years, and I still love her. Death cannot erase her smile from my memory or mute her quiet whistling that I hear plainly in my mind. It can't remove the vivid image I have of her wearing her flour-sack smock and pleated bonnet as she walked up the little country lane to the mailbox.

Love is stronger than death. I know because I can still taste the special flavor of Grandmother's mashed potatoes. I can smell the sweet, delicious aroma of her butterscotch pie baking in the old farmhouse kitchen. Nobody else's tasted just like hers. I can still see the sticks of gum and tiny handmade dolls that hung on the cedar Christmas tree in the front room.

Love is stronger than death. So, I must learn to be content to know that love is not affected by death—it doesn't end, it doesn't diminish, it doesn't change. Instead, love is immortalized and eternalized through death. And the possibility of that love ever being damaged or broken is eliminated forever. I'll put my trust in love, Lord.

In all these things we have full victory through
God who showed His love for us. Yes, I am
sure that nothing can separate us from the love
God has for us. Not death, not life, not angels,
not ruling spirits, nothing now, nothing in the
future, no powers, nothing above us, nothing
below us, or anything else in the whole world
will ever be able to separate us from the love of
God that is in Christ Jesus our Lord.

 Romans 8:37-39

Refocus

It's Friday night, Lord, and here I am alone again. I've worked all week, and now I'm ready to have a little fun, but I'm alone as usual. So, what shall I do this evening?

My house needs cleaning. I could vacuum and dust and change the sheets. Then, I could do the dishes, mop the floors and scrub the tubs. I like to clean house, but not on Friday night.

I could watch television. I've got three sets around the house to help drive away the loneliness. There's bound to be a good movie or a comedy to watch. Usually I enjoy a little TV before bedtime, but not on Friday night.

Maybe I should read a good book. That way, my mind can wander into another world, and I can pretend I'm someone else. Someone who's in love with life and has an exciting job in an exotic place. Someone who travels the fast lane of society and never has lonely Friday nights.

Perhaps I'll go shopping at the mall. I need a new sweater and a pair of shoes. I could grab a hot dog at one of the food stands in the mall. Most of the time I don't mind going shopping by myself, in fact, it's sort of fun, but not on Friday night.

Why am I doing this? I don't have to be alone on Friday night if I don't want to! I'll call somebody. I know, I'll call Charlotte and Barbara and Glenna and Linda. We'll go out to eat and to a movie. That way, none of us will be alone on Friday night. Why didn't I think of them sooner, instead of just thinking of me?

Every day is your opportu-
nity to begin again, to write a
new page in your book, to
renew your trust in God, to
eliminate the clutter of your
past, to reach out to others
with hope and help for the
future.

Sparky

Sparky, nicknamed for a comic-strip horse named Sparkplug, was a loser. He failed every subject in the eighth grade. Every subject! In high school he distinguished himself as the worst physics student in the school's history, receiving a flat zero in the course. He also flunked Latin, Algebra and English. He wasn't much good at sports either.

Sparky was socially awkward. The other kids didn't dislike him; they just didn't care about him one way or the other. He was shocked if a classmate said hello to him outside of school. In high school he never asked out a girl for fear of being turned down.

He was a loser, and everyone knew it, especially Sparky. He contented himself to be mediocre, except in one area. Sparky liked to draw. He was even proud of his own artwork. Of course, no one else appreciated it. In his senior year of high school, he submitted some cartoons to the class yearbook. Almost predictably, Sparky's drawings were rejected. Even so, Sparky trusted his instincts that drawing was his one natural talent, and he decided to be a professional artist.

After high school, Sparky wrote a letter to Walt Disney Studios explaining his qualifications to become a cartoonist for Disney. He received a form letter answer requesting samples of his artwork. So, Sparky drew the suggested cartoon scene, spending many hours to draw it just right. A job with Disney would be impressive, and there were many doubters to impress. Then, he sent his drawings and the form back to Disney. And he waited. Finally, the answer came and, you guessed it, Sparky didn't get the job.

So, Sparky decided to write his own autobiography in cartoons. He described his childhood as the little boy loser, the chronic underachiever, in a cartoon character the whole world now knows. For the boy who failed the entire eighth grade, the young artist whose work was rejected not only by Walt Disney Studios but by his own high school yearbook was "Sparky" Charles Monroe Schulz, better known to his fans as Charlie Brown.

Sparky's courage and faith in himself should inspire all of us. Even when no one else seems to have confidence in us or our abilities, we should trust ourselves, after all, who knows us better than we do.

If you must doubt, doubt your doubts—never your beliefs.

Brother John

Everyone just called him "Brother John." He was a small, gentle man with quiet words and twinkling smiles, but John Knox was a hero to many of us.

The doctor had told this 80-year-old man that his heart was growing weak and it was necessary for him to walk daily. So, every morning he walked with the sunrise from his home across town to a local hospital. Rain or shine, cold or hot, he trudged the six long miles. It was his "heart walk."

At the hospital information desk, he got a list of all the people who were members of the church he attended. Then, he went from room to room visiting. If a patient needed a newspaper, he went downstairs and bought them a paper. If they needed a cup of coffee, he went to the cafeteria and got it for them. If they wanted him to read to them, he read; pray with them, he prayed; talk to them, he talked. He tried to meet whatever need they had.

Brother John didn't stay long when he came to visit. He only came to help. If help was needed, he stayed. If it wasn't, he moved on to others who might need him. The doctors and nurses in the hospital came to respect and admire Brother

John for his quiet service and gentle care of their patients. And they grew to anticipate his daily visits with appreciation for they saw the smiles he left behind.

One of the local service organizations awarded Brother John a plaque as "Humanitarian of the Year." And he was so pleased. When it came time to accept the award, though, Brother John just blushed shyly and said, "I really did it just for me. It was my heart walk, you know." And everyone knew that it was, indeed, a walk of his heart.

Where'er I find the Good, the True, the Fair,
I ask no names—God's spirit dwelleth there!

S.T. Coleridge

Yesterday, Today and Forever

Yesterday was difficult, Lord. All I could do was flounder around in the past and be depressed. I just couldn't get it off my mind yesterday. It was as if a storm cloud hung over my heart from dawn until dusk. And the raindrops from that storm cloud splashed down my cheeks.

Today is better. The sun came up today in my heart. Who knows why? I don't really care why; I'm just glad it did. The world looks brighter today. I can feel Your presence more strongly today. I have renewed faith and trust today. My feet are a little lighter, and my eyes had a little twinkle in them this morning when I looked in the mirror. I'm okay, Lord. Thank You.

We can only appreciate the miracle of sunrise if we have waited in the darkness. The sun always rises.

*J*ust Today

I feel great today, Lord!
And I'm going to enjoy it just for today.

Today I'm not going to think about the past
and all the dreams that shattered.

Today I'm not going to plan for the future
or contemplate all the problems and
troubles that are bound to come.

Today I'm not going to consider how limited
my funds are or all the responsibilities
that are awaiting me.

Today I'm going to let my work go untouched
and my schedule unmet.

I feel great today, Lord!
And I'm going to enjoy it just for today.

The warp and woof of life is woven one day at a time. One day adds a strand of brightness and light. The next day adds a dark strand of shadows and depth. It is all the colors and hues together that create the masterpiece.

From the heart's most troubled moments come the courage and wisdom to build new happiness.

Anyone can smile when everything is going well. It's the person who can smile with tears streaming from eyes full of pain that deserves to be admired.

O God, have pity, for I am trusting You! I will hide beneath the shadow of Your wings, until the storm is past.

Psalm 57:1 KJV

But the Lord said to me, "My grace is enough for you. When you are weak, then My power is made perfect in you." So I am very happy to brag about my weaknesses. Then Christ's power can live in me. I am happy when I have weaknesses, insults, hard times, sufferings, and all kinds of troubles. All these things are for Christ. And I am happy, because when I am weak, then I am truly strong.

2 Corinthians 12:9-10

Pied Beauty

Glory be to God for dappled things—
For skies of couple-colour as a brinded cow;
For rose-moles all in stipple upon trout that swim;
Fresh-firecoal chestnut-falls; finche's wings;
Landscape plotted and pieced—fold, fallow and
plough;
And all trades, their gear and tackle and trim.

All things counter, original, spare, strange;
Whatever is fickle, freckled (who knows how?)
With swift, slow; sweet, sour; adazzle, dim;
He fathers-forth whose beauty is past change:
                                        Praise him.

                              Gerard Manley Hopkins

On the Move

I stood in the den of the big, four-bedroom house on Treasure Island watching people carry away our furniture and belongings one bit at a time. They loaded our things into pick-ups, station wagons, vans and trucks and drove away with them. And a bit of my heart left with each piece.

We were moving. Oh, I'd moved lots of times before as a preacher's daughter and a minister's wife. But this time was different. This time we were moving to New Zealand. This time we weren't taking our personal things with us. This time we couldn't drop back by to visit. This time was forever. We were going to be missionaries.

I stared out the kitchen window as the last folks drove away with my big, rolltop desk in the back of their pick-up. The house was practically empty. Just odds and ends remained for the final garage sale tomorrow. Dents in the shag carpet showed where the different pieces of furniture sat. Nails in the walls remained where paintings and knickknacks had hung.

I walked toward the back of the house and heard my footsteps resound through the vacant rooms. Crackerjack, our clownish parrot, squawked, "Fire! Fire!" and ran down the ladder in his cage to ring his bell. I smiled and scratched the top of his head thinking how I would miss his antics.

As I began packing one of my suitcases with clothes for the trip, I wondered what the new life overseas would be like.

I had been to New Zealand before on a month-long stay. I was familiar with their English traditions. I knew about their righthand-drive, tiny cars and mountain roads around Wellington. I knew about "high tea" and "low tea." I wasn't a total stranger in that foreign land. We even had good friends that lived in Wellington; so it wasn't as if I would be totally alone. But there were so many things I would miss.

No more hamburgers—my dietary staple. No more fried chicken, pizza or chocolate-fudge brownies. No more football games and footlong Coney Island hot dogs. No more iced tea or big shopping malls. No more large department stores and handy household gadgets. Life would be simpler there.

Well, maybe that wouldn't be so bad after all. Life had certainly been hectic here for the past few years. And New Zealand was an incredibly beautiful land. Surely I could learn to enjoy royal-blue water and white, sandy beaches. Surely I could learn to appreciate mid-afternoon snacks and hot drinks. And it wouldn't hurt me to do without brownies; shortbread cookies would be a good substitute anyway.

Besides, the Lord would be there, too. New Zealand was God's country, too. And I'd been there with Him before. I'd just trust Him to take care of everything else. He could handle it.

I closed the suitcase, locked it and set it on the floor. I had packed away my clothes...and my fears. I was ready to move on with the Lord. Then I smiled and walked to the kitchen for a big, chocolate brownie and a glass of iced tea.

What happens around us is largely outside our control, but how we choose to react
to it is inside our control. We can throw
our hands up in defeat or we can choose to
trust in God for His solution.

To The Autumnal Moon

Mild Splendour of the various-vested Night!
Mother of wildly-working visions! hail!
I watch thy gliding, while with watery light
Thy weak eye glimmers through a fleecy veil;
And when thou lovest thy pale orb to shroud
Behind the gathered blackness lost on high;
And when thou dartest from the windrent cloud
Thy placid lightning o'er the awakened sky.
Ah such is Hope! as changeful and as fair!
Now dimly peering on the wistful sight;
Now hid behind the dragon-winged Despair:
But soon emerging in her radiant might
She o'er the sorrow-clouded breast of Care
Sails, like a meteor kindling in its flight.

S.T. Coleridge

All we have willed or hoped or dreamed of good shall exist;
Not its semblance, but itself; no beauty, nor good, nor power
Whose voice has gone forth, but each survives for the melodist
When eternity affirms the conception of an hour.
The high that proved too high, the heroic for earth too hard,
The passion that left the ground to lose itself on the sky,
Are music sent up to God by the lover and the bard;
Enough that he heard it once: we shall hear it by-and-by.

 Robert Browning

*Therefore, my friend, you whom
I love and long for, my joy and
crown, stand firm in the
Lord, dear friend.*
Philippians 4:1 Adapted